SHARKS: HUNTERS of the DEEP™

THE GREAT WHITE SHARK

KING OF THE OCEAN

JOANNE RANDOLPH

PowerKiDS press
New York

Published in 2007 by The Rosen Publishing Group, Inc.
29 East 21st Street, New York, NY 10010

First Edition

Book Design: Greg Tucker and Dean Galiano
Photo Researcher: Sam Cha

Photo Credits: Cover © James D. Watt/SeaPics.com; pp. 4, 6, 10, 12, 14 © Digital Stock; p. 8 © Rob Stegmann; p. 16 © APF/Getty Images; p. 20 © Doug Perrine/SeaPics.com.

Library of Congress Cataloging-in-Publication Data

Randolph, Joanne.
The great white shark : king of the ocean / Joanne Randolph. — 1st ed.
p. cm. — (Sharks–hunters of the deep)
Includes bibliographical references and index.
ISBN-13: 978-1-4042-3624-0 (library binding : alk. paper)
ISBN-10: 1-4042-3624-4 (library binding : alk. paper)
1. White shark—Juvenile literature. I. Title.
QL638.95.L3R355 2007
597.3'3—dc22

2006019463

Manufactured in the United States of America

Contents

Meet the Great White

What is huge, has **gills** and a white belly, and is one of the deadliest hunters in the world? The answer is the great white shark, of course.

Imagine a nose with really sharp teeth swimming toward you. A great white's **skeleton** is made of the same thing that makes up your nose and ears. This special, bendable skeleton lets the shark move smoothly and quickly through the water. Let's find out more about the great white.

The great white shark can grow as long as 21 feet (6 m) and can weigh up to 7,000 pounds (3,175 kg). That's almost as much as two cars weigh!

The Great Gray Shark?

Because of its name, you might guess that the great white is white in color. Only the shark's belly is white, though. The top of the great white is bluish gray to grayish brown.

Sharks are fish, so they have fins and gills. Sharks do not have skin like other fish, though. Their very **rough** skin is covered with small, toothlike points. These points help the shark move quickly through water.

The great white is darker on the top and lighter on the bottom. This makes the shark hard to see from above and below.

GREAT WHITE JAWS

A Dentist's Dream

The great white's mouth is huge. It can be 16 inches (41 cm) across and is full of knife-sharp teeth. These teeth can be up to 3 inches (8 cm) long. Each tooth has an edge like a saw does. This allows the shark to easily cut through meat. In fact the great white's **jaws** are so powerful, and its teeth so sharp, that it can bite its **prey** in half!

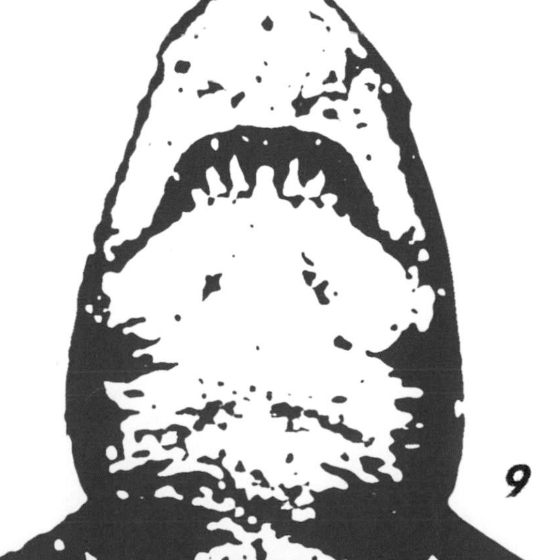

A great white can have up to 20 rows of teeth. As the teeth in front wear out, new ones move forward to take their place.

Great White Senses

Everything about the great white shark is made to help it hunt. The great white uses its outstanding eyesight to spot its prey. It also has the best sense of smell of all the sharks. A great white can smell blood from a hurt animal up to half a mile (.8 km) away. Great whites also use their sense of touch to help them hunt. They can feel very small movements in the water. This helps them find their next meal.

If there were just one drop of blood in a small swimming pool, a great white shark could smell it.

On the Hunt

The great white will eat almost anything. This includes dead fish and whales! However, its **favorite** foods are seals, sea lions, elephant seals, dolphins, and walruses. Great whites might like these foods because they are high in fat. This gives them the power they need to swim and hunt.

Unlike some other sharks, the great white hunts during the daytime. This causes one problem, though. Sometimes great whites are hunting when people are swimming.

Sea lions are one of the great white's favorite foods.

Danger to People

The great white shark is one of the most-feared sharks in the world. In many places it is called "man-eater" or "white death." In truth, this shark does not really look for people as prey. However, great whites' hunting grounds are often the same places where people like to **surf** and swim.

Great white **attacks** might simply be a mistake. Surfers and swimmers have the same basic shape as the shark's favorite foods.

Fewer than 100 shark attacks on people are reported each year. When the great white is ready to attack, it pushes its nose up and its jaws forward to bite its prey.

An Important Part to Play

You might not want a great white as a friend. However, great white sharks play an important part in keeping the ocean healthy. They feed on hurt and dead animals. They also keep the number of fish and other animals down.

The great white is at the top of the **food chain**. This means it has few enemies. Killer whales and larger sharks sometimes eat great whites. The great white has the most to fear from people, though.

People fish for great white sharks to get their skins, jawbones, livers, fins, and their meat. People also hunt great whites for sport or out of fear.

Places Where Great
Whites Live

Home Is Where the Food Is

You might wonder where the great white shark lives. The great white spends much of its time swimming along the coasts of most **continents**. It favors places where the water is not too hot or too cold.

Great whites are found in the waters around North America, Australia, Japan, the northern coast of Africa, and in the Mediterranean Sea, among other places. The surest way to find a great white is to look where its favorite foods live.

The great white likes to swim around small islands and other places where seals and sea lions live. The places in red on this map are where great whites can be found.

Great White Babies

The great white starts out as an egg inside its mother's body. **Female** great whites have babies only a few times in their life. They carry up to nine eggs inside their bodies for a year or more. The mother then gives birth to live pups. Each pup can be nearly 5 feet (1.5 m) long when it is born. The babies will have no help from their mother once they are born. They are on their own.

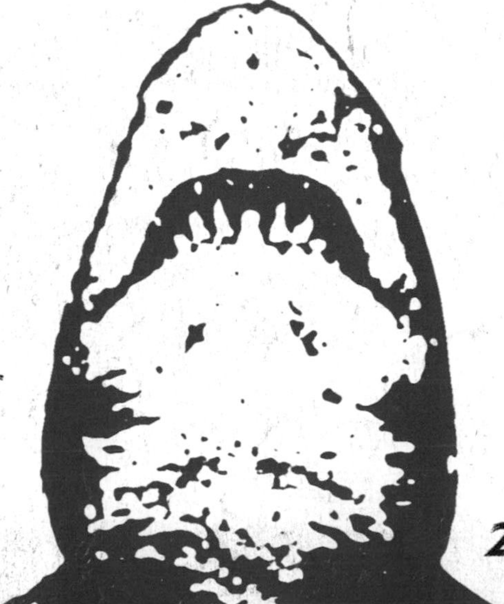

No one knows just how long great white sharks live. They live at least 14 years, though they likely live much longer.

Keeping the Great White Safe

Did you know that the great white shark needs your help? You might not think that a shark like the great white needs any **protection**. However, it takes a long time for the number of sharks to grow. People have caught too many great whites, so they have become **endangered**. Great whites are one of 50 shark **species** that are endangered. By learning more about great whites, people can learn to respect this great hunter rather than fear it.

GLOSSARY

attacks (uh-TAKS) Acts of trying to hurt someone or something.

continents (KON-teh-nents) Earth's seven large landmasses. They are Africa, Antarctica, Asia, Australia, Europe, North America, and South America.

endangered (in-DAYN-jerd) Describing an animal whose species or group has almost all died out.

favorite (FAY-vuh-rut) Most liked.

female (FEE-mayl) Having to do with women and girls.

food chain (FOOD CHAYN) Living things that are each other's food.

gills (GILZ) Body parts that fish use for breathing.

jaws (JAHZ) Bones in the top and bottom of the mouth.

prey (PRAY) An animal that is hunted by another animal for food.

protection (pruh-TEK-shun) Something that keeps something else from being hurt.

rough (RUF) Not smooth.

skeleton (SKEH-leh-tun) What gives an animal's or a person's body its shape.

species (SPEE-sheez) One kind of living thing. All people are one species.

surf (SERF) To ride the ocean waves using one's body or a special board.

INDEX

WEB SITES

Due to the changing nature of Internet links, PowerKids Press has developed an online list of Web sites related to the subject of this book. This site is updated regularly. Please use this link to access the list:
www.powerkidslinks.com/sharks/grwhite/